DIEGO:

DREAM BIG
AND BELIEVE —!

Frieda B. Herself

by Renata Bowers
pictures by Michael Chesworth

Dream your dreams big and believe they can be.

To Ann, for introducing me to Frieda.
To Jennie, for always believing in her.
And to David, Hunter and Garreth,
for making her part of the family.

First edition, 2010
Library of Congress Control Number: 2009913921
ISBN 978-0-9843862-3-9
Printed in the United States.

To visit Frieda and/or order additional
copies of Frieda B. Herself, go to
www.friedab.com.

W ay up in the village of Fiddle-Dee-Dee

on the corner of
   Beechwood and Hickory streets
in a purple brick house,
   number three-thirty-three,

lives the world's biggest dreamer...

...her name's Frieda B.

Frieda B. has got
    wirey, firey hair
and she rarely wears shoes
    'cause she likes her feet bare.

She has speckles of freckles
all over her nose
and she takes her dog, Zilla,
wherever she goes.

Like you and like me, Frieda B.'s free to be
    anyone, anywhere that she dreams she can be.
So she dreams her dreams big, some as big as the ocean,
    and fills them with color and music and motion.

By slipping-on flippers
and making a wish,
she can breathe underwater
and talk to the fish.

She can zoom to the moon,
    she can swing from the stars,
she can polka on Pluto
    with Martians from Mars.

She can shrink herself down to the size of a pea
so the plant in her window is big as a tree.

And whenever her purple brick house gets too loud,
Frieda B. takes a long, quiet nap on a cloud.

Frieda travels to lands you won't find on a map,
    like Planet Mandoo where they hoot and they clap
and they giggle and wiggle
    and laugh 'til they're red
if you tell a good joke
    and you stand on your head.

The places she visits are her own creation.
She gets there by using her imagination.
Sometimes she stands high on the top of her bed,
grabs her sheets like two reins and yells...

"Watch out ahead!"

But one summer night,
snuggled up in her bed,
Frieda found that she hadn't
one dream in her head.

Her mom and her dad
had both kissed her goodnight,
and they'd wished her sweet dreams
as they'd turned out her light.

But the dreams wouldn't come,
and as hard as she tried,
Frieda B. could not find
even one dream inside.

She pummeled her pillow with pent-up frustration and cried, *"I've outgrown it—my imagination!"*

Then *poof!*—from her pillow
shot feathers in flight.
Frieda sat up, and watched them,
and to her delight
they drifted as bird shadows
high on her wall,
joining roosters and horses
and cows in a stall.

Frieda followed those birds to a magical farm
   where the animals sang as they danced arm-in-arm.
She joined in their jig and they all had such fun,
   the moon had to scold them for waking the sun.

At dawn, as she bid
    fond farewell to new friends,
Frieda B. the big dreamer
    was happy again.

For those feathers had taught her:
When dreams will not budge,
they're really not lost—
they just need a good nudge.

So if you hear a *"whoosh!"* past your window one night,
don't be scared—it is probably Frieda in flight,
on her way to Mandoo or the land of Away-sis,
or one of a jillion more make-believe places.

Frieda B.'s a big dreamer, that's certainly true,
　　but the world's biggest dreamer is also in you.
All the color and music inside—set it free.
　　Just dream your dreams big and believe they can be.

And if, as you dream, you should happen to meet
　　a feisty young girl with red hair and bare feet,
you'll talk and you'll laugh
　　and you'll dream and you'll see:
　　　　You don't have to be Frieda...

...to be free-to-be.